DOLLAR STORE DANNY

and the Salt Shaker Spaceship

An AudioCraft Publishing, Inc. book

This book is a work of fiction. Names, places, characters and incidents are used fictitiously, or are products of the author's very active imagination.

Book storage and warehouses provided by *Chillermania* ©
Indian River, Michigan

Dollar $tore Danny and the Salt Shaker Spaceship
Copyright © 2018 by Johnathan Rand/AudioCraft Publishing, Inc.
ISBN: 978-1-893699-41-0

Librarians/Media Specialists:
PCIP/MARC records available **free of charge** at
www.americanchillers.com

Illustrations by Michal Jacot © 2018 AudioCraft Publishing, Inc.
Cover/interior layout and graphics design by Howard Roark

Printed in USA

The
Salt Shaker
Spaceship

VISIT CHILLERMANIA!

WORLD HEADQUARTERS FOR BOOKS BY JOHNATHAN RAND!

Yooperland

Indian River

Alpena

Traverse City

MICHIGAN

Mt. Pleasant

Bay City

Grand Rapids

Lansing

Detroit

Kalamazoo

CHILLERMANIA!

***I-75 Exit 313
then south
1 mile!***

Visit the HOME for books by Johnathan Rand! Featuring books, hats, shirts, bookmarks and other cool stuff not available anywhere else in the world! Plus, watch the American Chillers website for news of special events and signings at *CHILLERMANIA!* with author Johnathan Rand! Located in northern lower Michigan, on I-75! Take exit 313 . . . then south 1 mile! For more info, call (231) 238-0338. And be afraid! Be veeeery afraaaaaaiiiid . . . .

Chapter One

On Friday, Danny and his mother went shopping at the dollar store. Danny's mother looked for things she needed.

But almost always, Danny found himself in trouble.

"Danny, will you do me a favor?" his mother asked.

Danny nodded. "Yes," he said.

Danny's mother pointed to a shelf. "Go over there and see if you can find some paper cups. I need to find a few other things over here."

"Okay," Danny said.

Danny walked to where his mother was pointing.

He looked for paper cups.

He did not see any.

But he did find something else. Something that caught his attention. Something that looked cool.

A glass salt shaker.

Danny picked it up. He rolled it over in his hand.

"This looks just like a tiny spaceship," he said to himself.

Danny closed his eyes and thought very, very hard.

He wished he had his own spaceship. He would explore outer space and other planets. He would blast through space at the speed of light. He would sail among the stars! He would have so much fun!

Danny opened his eyes.

"Holy cow!" Danny said as he looked around.

The salt shaker had turned into a spaceship!

Chapter Two

Danny was now seated inside the salt shaker. But it was not a salt shaker anymore. It had turned into a real spaceship! There was a control panel in front of him. It had lots of blinking lights and buttons. There were handlebars to steer the craft. On the control panel was a red button with two words:

BLAST OFF

Danny thought about pressing the button.

"No," he said. "I had better not. It might be very dangerous."

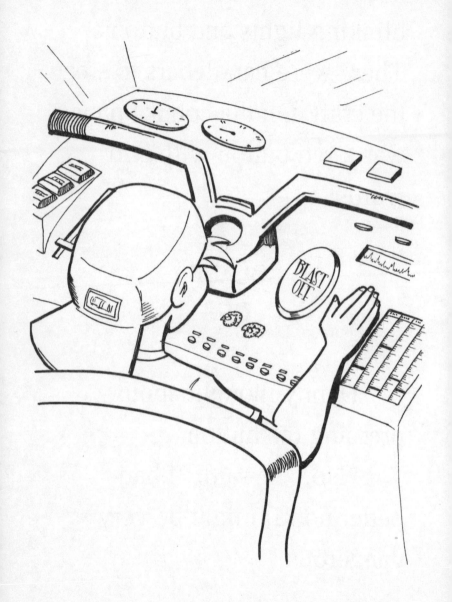

Danny looked around. Through the glass, he could see the items on the shelves inside the dollar store. No one else was around.

"Well," Danny said. He smiled. "Maybe I *will* try it. Maybe it will be fun."

Danny pressed the button.

There was a loud roar.

The spacecraft trembled.

Danny was very scared. He looked for a button to shut

off the spaceship. He did not find one.

Then, on its own, the salt shaker spaceship rose from the floor. Danny and the salt shaker spaceship were going to crash into the ceiling!

Oh, no!

Chapter Three

Danny closed his eyes. He held on tight to the handle-bars.

The salt shaker spaceship shook. Then, there was a loud crash.

Danny opened his eyes.
He could not believe what he
saw.

He was no longer in the dollar store! All around him there were stars and the deep, dark black of space.

"Oh, man!" Danny said. "I think I blasted off into outer space!"

It was true. Danny was seated inside his salt shaker spaceship, speeding through space. He passed many stars and planets.

Then, he saw something

else.

Ahead of him, he saw another spaceship. It looked like a giant ketchup bottle.

Inside the giant ketchup bottle were strange-looking creatures.

The creatures looked at Danny.

Danny looked at the creatures.

The creatures looked angry.

"Look!" one of the creatures said. He pointed at Danny. "It's a human boy! Let's capture him and make a sandwich. He would taste yummy!"

Once again, Danny knew that he was in a lot of trouble.

Chapter Four

Danny held the handlebars
and turned the spacecraft. He
blasted off in the other
direction. But the aliens
followed! They shot at him
with lasers! Some of the

lasers nearly hit his salt shaker spaceship!

Up ahead, Danny saw a large, red planet.

"I think that is Mars," said Danny. He looked around. The only other things he saw were millions of stars.

Behind him, the alien spaceship was getting closer. Laser beams blasted all around his salt shaker space-ship.

Danny was very worried. He knew that his spaceship might get hit by a laser beam.

Then, Danny heard a voice. It came from a speaker inside his salt shaker spaceship.

"Captain Danny," the voice said. "You must get away from the aliens and return to the dollar store."

"I'm trying!" Danny said. "But they're shooting at me!"

Behind Danny, the alien spacecraft was getting closer.

"I'm hungry," one of the creatures said.

"We must capture the human boy," one of the aliens said. He rubbed his tummy. "He will make a very tasty sandwich."

Danny was now more frightened than ever. Using the handlebars, he turned the salt shaker spaceship.

Then, a laser beam hit! The salt shaker spaceship rocked and wobbled. An alarm siren screamed inside the craft.

"Oh, no!" shouted Danny. "Oh, no! This is a disaster!"

Chapter Five

"My spaceship is hit!" Danny screamed.

Ahead of him, in space, Danny saw something glowing among the stars.

It was the dollar store!

"I've got to make it!" Danny shouted. "I can't let those aliens get me!"

Danny held tightly to the handlebars. He tried to control his salt shaker spaceship. He tried to steer it toward the dollar store.

Behind him, the alien spaceship was getting closer and closer.

Up ahead, the dollar store was getting closer.

"I'm going to make it!" Danny shouted.

"Stop him!" one of the aliens cried. "We must catch him before he escapes!"

"I'm starving!" said one of the aliens.

Danny was very scared. He did not want to be captured by the aliens. He did not want to be a sandwich.

"Captain Danny!" a voice boomed from the speaker

inside the salt shaker spaceship. "Use the pedal on the
floor! It will make you go
faster!"

With his right foot,
Danny pressed the pedal on
the floor.

The salt shaker spaceship
went faster.

He pressed the pedal
harder.

The salt shaker spaceship
went even *faster*.

The aliens were still behind him. They were still chasing him in their ketchup bottle spaceship.

Danny and his salt shaker spaceship were getting closer and closer to the dollar store in space.

But there was one very big problem.

Danny did not know how to make the spaceship slow down.

"Help!" Danny shouted.

But it was too late. Danny closed his eyes as his space-ship crashed into the dollar store.

Chapter Six

Danny opened his eyes. He was standing in the dollar store, holding the salt shaker.

He was not in space.

There were no aliens chasing him.

"Wow," Danny said with a sigh. "That was scary."

He heard a noise behind him. He gasped. He knew it must be the aliens!

Danny spun.

It was not an alien.

It was his mother.

"There you are," Danny's mother said. "Did you find the paper cups?"

Danny shook his head. "No," he said.

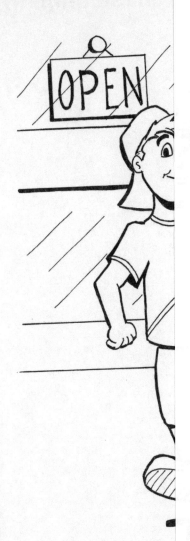

"Come on," said Danny's mother. "It's time to go."

"I went to outer space!" Danny said to his mother. "I was chased by aliens!"

"That's nice," Danny's mother said. She held out her hand. "I'm glad you are safe. Put that salt shaker on the shelf, and let's go home."

Danny returned the salt shaker to the shelf. He took his mother's hand, and they left the dolla~~r store.~~

"Outer s~~pace was~~

Danny said t~~o his mother.~~

"I'm sure it was,~~"~~

mother said ~~with a smile.~~

As they ~~got in the car,~~

Danny drea~~med about~~

back to the ~~dollar store.~~

dreamed ab~~out flying~~

exciting, cr~~azy adventures.~~

great books by Johnathan Rand!

Michigan Chillers:

#1: Mayhem on Mackinac Island
#2: Terror Stalks Traverse City
#3: Poltergeists of Petoskey
#4: Aliens Attack Alpena
#5: Gargoyles of Gaylord
#6: Strange Spirits of St. Ignace
#7: Kreepy Klowns of Kalamazoo
#8: Dinosaurs Destroy Detroit
#9: Sinister Spiders of Saginaw
#10: Mackinaw City Mummies
#11: Great Lakes Ghost Ship
#12: AuSable Alligators
#13: Gruesome Ghouls of Grand Rapids
#14: Bionic Bats of Bay City
#15: Calumet Copper Creatures
#16: Catastrophe in Caseville
#17: A Ghostly Haunting in Grand Haven
#18: Sault Ste. Marie Sea Monsters
#19: Drummond Island Dogman
#20: Lair of the Lansing Leprechauns

Freddie Fernortner, Fearless First Grader:

#1: The Fantastic Flying Bicycle
#2: The Super-Scary Night Thingy
#3: A Haunting We Will Go
#4: Freddie's Dog Walking Service
#5: The Big Box Fort
#6: Mr. Chewy's Big Adventure
#7: The Magical Wading Pool
#8: Chipper's Crazy Carnival
#9: Attack of the Dust Bunnies from Outer Space!
#10: The Pond Monster
#11: Tadpole Trouble
#12: Frankenfreddie
#13: Day of the Dinosaurs

American Chillers Double Thrillers:
Vampire Nation &
Attack of the Monster Venus Melon

Dollar $tore Danny:
#1: The Dangerous Dinosaur
#2: The Salt Shaker Spaceship
#3: The Crazy Crayons

Adventure Club series:
#1: Ghost in the Graveyard
#2: Ghost in the Grand
#3: The Haunted Schoolhouse

order on line at:
www.americanchillers.com

For Teens:
PANDEMIA: A novel of the
bird flu and the end of the world
(written with Christopher Knight)

USA